AFRICAN STORIES ABOUT THE TORTOISE

Written and Adapted by
Ernest & Madge Ikpe

AuthorHouse™
1663 Liberty Drive
Bloomington, IN 47403
www.authorhouse.com
Phone: 1-800-839-8640

First published by AuthorHouse 08/11/2011

ISBN: 978-1-4634-2726-9 (sc)

Library of Congress Control Number: 2011910159

Printed in the United States of America

Any people depicted in stock imagery provided by Thinkstock are models,
and such images are being used for illustrative purposes only.
Certain stock imagery © Thinkstock.

This book is printed on acid-free paper.

Because of the dynamic nature of the Internet, any web addresses or links contained in this book may have changed
since publication and may no longer be valid. The views expressed in this work are solely those of the author and do not
necessarily reflect the views of the publisher, and the publisher hereby disclaims any responsibility for them.

authorHOUSE®

AFRICAN STORIES ABOUT THE TORTOISE

Written and Adapted by Ernest & Madge Ikpe

Illustrated By: Nsisong Augustine Ukut

COPYRIGHT WARNING

A LEGEND

A legend is a story that tells about extraordinary acts. The tortoise in these stories is able to do some extraordinary acts.

African legend believes that the tortoise is the cleverest, trickiest and most cunning of all the animals. Parents tell African folktales to their children in the evenings after dinner.

Every African folktale/story usually has a moral, or lesson, and this is why we decided to have these stories available to children of all ages. We hope they will enjoy them, and learn from the lessons that are in them. These are animal stories about people.

Folktale —A story that has no known author, and was originally passed down from one generation to another by word of mouth. It is usually about ordinary people, or animals that act like people.

<u>DEDICATION</u>

My grandparents and parents told me many stories after dinner most evenings, when I was a child, and I was enthralled by the stories about the Tortoise.

These stories are dedicated to our grandchildren, Essien, Annietie (Annie), and Vincent.

May they have many enjoyable imaginative hours reading these stories, and sharing them with their friends.

Ernest Ikpe

<u>PROLOGUE</u> *

<u>The Tortoise Enters and Speaks</u>

This world was made for all creatures

The big, the small, the strong, the weak

The tall, the short, the smart and the not so smart.

The world then becomes a place

For the survival of the fittest.

To be fit, then, means that one has to use

Either one's size or one's brains.

Since I am small, I use my brains.

*An introductory speech to an event or play.

READ ON !

The Tortoise and the Pig

The tortoise was lazy and never worked hard. Because he was so lazy, he had little money or no money, and he always had money problems.

The pig was the opposite of the tortoise. He worked hard, saved his money, and had no money problems.

One day, the tortoise went to the pig for a loan. At first, the pig refused to lend tortoise any money because the pig did not know how the tortoise would pay back, since he was very lazy and did not like to work. So tortoise told the pig that he was expecting a big money reward from his investments, and he convinced the pig to give him the loan. The pig reluctantly gave tortoise the loan.

Many months passed and the tortoise did not pay, so the pig went to the tortoise and asked him for his money. The tortoise told him, "Come back in two days' time and

I will pay you."

Meanwhile, the tortoise was thinking of a plan, and he told his wife that he was expecting the pig. "You should use my belly as a grinding stone for your corn." (A grinding stone is used in Africa to grind grain and it looks rough like the belly of a tortoise). Tortoise told his wife, "You should say nothing to the pig when he comes, and you should not answer his questions."

When the pig went to tortoise's house, he saw tortoise's wife grinding corn to prepare a meal. The pig asked, "Where is your husband?" She did not answer but continued grinding her corn. The pig asked her "Did your husband leave any money with you for me?" She did not answer.

With annoyance, the pig picked up what he thought was a grinding stone and threw it away into the nearest bush. Because of this, a quarrel started between Mrs.

Tortoise and the pig. While this was going on, Tortoise appeared and the pig quickly demanded his money. The tortoise replied, "I tied the money to my wife's grinding stone for safety." Then he turned to his wife and asked for the stone. "Mr. Pig threw it away because he was annoyed," was her answer. Mr. Tortoise turned to the pig and told him, "Look for the stone and you will find your money."

The pig went into the bush and started digging all over, looking for the stone, which he would never find, because the stone was in fact Mr. Tortoise himself.

This is the reason the pig digs the ground until today, looking for the Tortoise's grinding stone.

Lesson: "You Should Neither Be A Borrower Nor a Lender."

The Tortoise, the Elephant and the Hippopotamus

The elephant and the hippopotamus were always laughing at the tortoise because the tortoise is very small. One day, elephant said to tortoise, "I can smash you into pieces with my feet." The hippopotamus said, "I can smash you into pieces with my big head."

The tortoise was not happy. He thought for a long time about what he should do to embarrass the elephant and the hippopotamus. So one day, he went to the elephant and told him that he was challenging the elephant to a tug-of-war contest on a date they should fix. (A tug-of-war is a contest of strength in which two teams pull on opposite ends of a rope, each team trying to pull the other across a dividing line.)

The elephant laughed at the tortoise and asked him, "Are you serious about this challenge?" The tortoise said, "Yes!" So they agreed on a date for the challenge. Tortoise told the elephant, "On that day, I will come with a rope for you and while you are at one end, I will be at the other end." A friend would give a signal for them to start pulling.

The tortoise also went to the hippopotamus and told him that he was challenging him to a tug-of-war contest on a date that they should fix. Hippopotamus also laughed and asked, "Are you serious about this challenge?" Again tortoise answered, "Yes!"

Hippopotamus agreed on the same date that the elephant agreed on for the challenge. So tortoise told hippopotamus, "On that date, I will come with a rope for you, and while you are at one end, I will be at the other end." A friend would give a signal for them to start pulling. On the fixed date, the tortoise, carrying a long rope, went to the elephant. He gave one end of the rope to the elephant, and said, "Here, take this end." He went to the hippopotamus who could not see the elephant because of the long distance. He gave him the other end, and said, "Here, take this end." Neither the elephant nor the hippopotamus knew that each of them had one end of the rope. Then the tortoise went to the middle of the distance between both animals and shook the rope as a signal for both to start pulling. The elephant and hippopotamus could not see tortoise because he was so small. They pulled for hours while the tortoise watched, but they did not succeed in pulling each other across the line.

The elephant began to wonder how the tortoise could be so strong that he could not to be pulled across the line. So, the hippopotamus decided to find out if indeed it was the tortoise that was at the other end of the rope. Both animals were surprised to find out that the tortoise had tricked them by having them pull against each other. Hippopotamus shouted, "So he tricked us!"

The elephant and the hippopotamus planned to go to tortoise's home to confront him. "Let us go to his house," said elephant. "Let us go," said hippopotamus.

When the elephant and the hippopotamus got to tortoise's house, it was now tortoise's turn to laugh at them. Tortoise told them that he could make them do anything, at anytime, because they were only big and fat for nothing. "I am small, but I am smart." Both animals finally left with a promise to outsmart tortoise another time.

Lesson: Give respect to people and they will respect you. Do not make fun of people who are not as big as you.

The Tortoise and the Hare

The hare is known to be a fast runner. He is friendly, and it is easy to make friend with him. His only problem is that he falls asleep at any time.

It was not difficult for the tortoise to become friendly with the hare. They were seen together everywhere all the time. Even though hare and tortoise were friends, the hare used to tell tortoise that he, the hare, could run faster than tortoise. The tortoise was not happy to be told over and over again that he could not outrun the hare.

After several days, the tortoise, still annoyed with the hare, made a suggestion that they should go for a day of cross-town running race against each other to see who would win. The hare readily accepted, confident that he would win. They both agreed upon a date, time and place for the race.

The tortoise went home and planned how he would defeat the hare in the race. He went to a friend, the soldier ant, and gave him money to organize a party for the rest of their friends.
"You must invite the hare too," said the tortoise.
The party was held in the morning of the race in soldier ant's house. Everyone was there: everyone including the ape, the elephant, the giraffe, the hippopotamus, the monkey, the snake and the tiger.

They ate and drank until they were too full. The hare stuffed himself also. The tortoise pretended to be eating and drinking but in fact, he did not eat or drink.

After partying for a long time, everybody left, and so did the tortoise and the hare. But the time for the race was near, so the tortoise left the party to go to the race. The hare followed later, but he was dragging himself very slowly because he was too full.

Now it was time for the race. The race started and the hare ran like the wind, leaving behind the tortoise. The hare continued to run, with the tortoise following far behind.

Soon, the hare felt tired and sleepy and decided to stop and take a short nap because he knew that the tortoise was too slow to catch up with him. But the hare slept longer than he wanted, and when he woke up to continue the race, the tortoise was at the finishing line waiting for him.

The tortoise won the marathon and he collected a prize that was meant for the winner.

The hare left with an unhappy memory.

Lesson: Do not be lazy. Work hard and steady and you will succeed
          Slow and steady wins the race.

The Tortoise and the King's Daughter

Once upon a time, there was a King who had a beautiful daughter. Anybody who wanted to marry his daughter had to pass a difficult test that the King himself made up. Many failed to complete the tests, and others even died.

Tortoise heard about the King and his daughter, and he heard that those who wanted to marry the daughter had to pass a test. The tortoise thought about his chances, and finally went to the King.

When the tortoise saw the King, the tortoise explained, "I have come to propose marriage to you daughter, Your Majesty. "

The King looked down at the tortoise and laughed for a while before he said, "Just looking at you, I can tell that you are not qualified to marry my daughter."

"Why have you come to that conclusion, my King?"

The King replied, "You are not only short, but ugly as well. Also, you will not be able to pass the test that I will give you."

The tortoise begged the King to allow his daughter to see him to decide for herself about his qualities.

"Before I allow you to see my daughter, you will also have to pass a test first," was the King's reply.

Each person who wanted to marry the King's daughter had a different test and the King told tortoise that for his test, he was to stay overnight in a room full of biting mosquitoes.

"If you pass my test, you will marry the princess," the King said.

The tortoise left and went home to plan how he would overcome the mosquitoes' bites.

When the tortoise returned to the King's palace the next day, he found out that a room full of mosquitoes was ready for his test. He was to stay in that room all night. A guard and a dog stood at the door to make sure that the tortoise stayed in the room all night.

As soon as the tortoise entered the room, mosquitoes started buzzing around him. To put his plan to work, tortoise called the dog, "Come here, I want to know why I am here," as if he did not know. The dog informed him, "You must pass the mosquito test before you can see the princess."

"What test?" asked tortoise.

"You must not kill the mosquitoes by using your hands to kill them." At this, the dog thoughtlessly demonstrated by using his paw to hit imaginary mosquitoes on his body. This is what tortoise was expecting him to do.

Using his plan, the tortoise started to sing.

"I am the most beautiful person in the world. I am bald and have no hair on my head."

While he was singing, tortoise used his hand (pretending only to touch his head) to drive away the mosquitoes but he was really killing them. "I have a beautiful nose." (As he touched his nose, he drove away and killed the mosquitoes.) The tortoise sang and described different parts of his body around which the mosquitoes were buzzing. (He brushed every part of his body that he mentioned in his song to drive away and kill the mosquitoes before they could bite him.)

The tortoise sang, danced and jumped about all night and the guard was peeping through a peep hole in the door and watching in amazement, wondering if the tortoise was mad. He did not realize that tortoise was actually killing the mosquitoes as he danced and jumped about.

When it was daylight, the King called the guard and asked the guard if the tortoise was alive or dead. The guard replied, "I have never seen anyone like that who could sing and dance all night, my Lord. Yes, my Lord, he is still alive. He must have put a spell on the mosquitoes."

The door to the room opened, and the tortoise came out unharmed by the mosquitoes. Instead, all the mosquitoes were dead. The King was surprised because he never expected the tortoise to live and be able to marry his daughter. But to keep his promise, the King allowed tortoise to marry his daughter. So, tortoise and the King's daughter lived happily ever after, together.

Lesson: Never think that you are smarter than the next person.
         Give respect to everyone.

The Tortoise and His Jealous Friends

The tortoise has always claimed that he was the King of all the animals. His friends usually ignored him and became annoyed with him because of his boastful insistence. His friends met secretly and planned to put an end to the tortoise's boastings.

After a long discussion, they decided that the tortoise should be thrown into a ditch and covered up with sand and left to die.

They finally invited the tortoise to a party near the covered ditch. Just before the party was to end, the tortoise was held, taken and thrown into the ditch. He was informed that he was being punished for his continuous boastings and claiming to be king of them all. When they started to cover the ditch with sand, the tortoise in turn started to jump on top of each pile so that he would not be covered by the sand.

This continued until the ditch was full of sand. Little did the other animals know that the tortoise was almost on top of the sand and the ditch. When all the animals left, singing and laughing, the tortoise crawled out. He went home and told his family what happened.

According to his plan, the family went around the village to ask other animals if they knew where the King was. Everyone denied knowing anything about the tortoise who was not the "King" anyway.

By design, the tortoise did not leave his house for several days. When he finally walked out of his house, all the other animals started to run away shouting. Some were shouting, "The king is alive." Others were shouting, "The tortoise is not dead," while the rest were shouting that the tortoise had risen. They all thought that the tortoise was out for a revenge; rather, when the commotion ended, he called all of them together and told them that he was not angry with them because none of them could do him any harm. On the other hand, he demanded an apology from them within two days, because of their cowardly actions, or there would be disaster coming to them. After saying so, he went home and the rest of the animals met and discussed what action to take. Many of them were annoyed with the decision to kill the tortoise in the first place. A few others suggested that they should present gifts to the tortoise to make him happy and that they should not wait for the two days as demanded by the tortoise. Finally, they all agreed that by noon the following day, they should go to the tortoise's house to play drums, dance and be merry and give gifts. They did that the following day and told the tortoise that indeed he was their King.

Lesson: Never plan any evil act against your friend or your enemy. Love your neighbor as yourself.

THE EPILOGUE *

The Tortoise Speaks

Who Do You Think I am?
Forget about What They Say About Him, The Lion
Forget about What They Say About Him, The Elephant
Forget about What They Say About Him, The Monkey
Or The Snake, the Snail and the Rest.

What You Should Not Forget Is That
I Am the King of All.
I Am Smart and Knowledgeable
I Am A Philosopher, I Think While I Walk Slowly.

I Can Get What I Want,
When I Want It, and From Whom I Want It.

I Can Live On Land and In the Water
How Many of Us (Animals) Can Live Like That?

That Is Why I Am the One and Only King!

I AM THE KING

*A short speech spoken directly to the audience after the end of a story.

CPSIA information can be obtained
at www.ICGtesting.com
Printed in the USA
256309LV00003B

9 781463 427269